SABAN'S POWER RANGERS SAMURAI™

ARMED FOR BATTLE

By Ace Landers

SCHOLASTIC INC.

New York   Toronto   London   Auckland
Sydney   Mexico City   New Delhi   Hong Kong

ISBN 978-0-545-39010-1

12 11 10 9 8 7 6 5 4 3 2 1   12 13 14 15 16/0

Printed in the U.S.A.
First printing, January 2012

40

*F*or hundreds of years, monsters called Nighloks have crept out of the Netherworld and into our world. Their goal is always the same— to cause mayhem and destruction.

But we have heroes to defend us—the Samurai Power Rangers. They have mysterious powers that have been passed down from parent to child for generations.

The Rangers live among us, training for the time when they will be called upon to save the world.

The leader of the Nighloks is the evil Master Xandred. Trapped in the Netherworld, he dreams of destroying all humans— especially the Power Rangers.

With the help of Octoroo, one of his followers, Master Xandred hatched a wicked plan.

"As legend has it," said Octoroo, "every time something terrible happens on earth, the water level in the Sanzu River rises from all the tears of the crybaby humans. If we keep scaring the humans, the river will rise so high that we can sail out of the Netherworld forever!"

"That plan might work. I'm glad I thought of it!" roared Master Xandred. "Scorpionic, get over here!"

Scorpionic, a Nighlok with a dangerous tail, rose from the Sanzu River and climbed aboard Master Xandred's boat.

"Master, you rang?" said Scorpionic.

Suddenly, the Gap Sensor at the Shiba House blared a warning. The alarm meant that a Nighlok had come through a cosmic gap from the Netherworld.

The Samurai Power Rangers had a new battle to fight!

The Gap Sensor was right! Scorpionic and the Moogers were terrorizing the town.

"Don't scare the humans all at once," yelled Scorpionic. "Slowly corner them. That will be more fun."

Everything was going according to Master Xandred's plan until the Power Rangers came to the rescue.

"Samuraizer!" shouted the Power Rangers as they began to morph. "Go, go, Samurai!"

"Rangers together, Samurai forever!"

"Attack!" commanded Scorpionic. The Moogers charged forward to destroy the Power Rangers.

The Blue Ranger blasted two Moogers with his powerful Hydro Bow.

Using her special Sky Fan, the Pink Ranger slashed and hacked her way through the army of Moogers.

The Green Ranger was surrounded by Moogers, but he had his Forest Spear. He whipped the spear round and round. With explosive fury, he wiped out some of the Moogers.

The Red Ranger used his Fire Smasher to thrash and trash the remaining Moogers. But would the Fire Smasher help him defeat Scorpionic?

Scorpionic charged forward to take down the Red Ranger.

"It's crunch time!" said Scorpionic. Then he sent the Red Ranger crashing into a building.

Now that the Red Ranger was out of the way, Scorpionic turned his attention to the other Rangers.

"Bye-bye, Power Rangers," laughed Scorpionic. Then he unleashed his Whirlwind Scythe Attack!

The Power Rangers were struck down by Scorpionic's massive power.

"Like taking candy from a baby!" said Scorpionic.

Though injured, the Red Ranger rose to his feet. He said, "Stand up, Rangers! We either defeat the Nighlok or be defeated. Stay strong."

The Red Ranger's determination surprised Scorpionic. The Nighlok was quickly knocked down by the strength of the Fire Smasher.

Then the other Power Rangers took their chance to destroy Scorpionic.

Using the Spin Sword Quintuple Slash, the Power Rangers struck again. Scorpionic exploded into flames!

But it takes more than that to defeat a Nighlok. Each Nighlok has two lives. Its second life is as a giant MegaMonster that towers over the city.
"Don't think you've won just yet, Rangers!" screeched Scorpionic.

"Looks like we're not done yet," said the Red
Ranger. "We need Mega Mode Power. Let's go!"

The Rangers morphed their Folding-Zords into gigantic vehicles to combat the MegaMonster.

But Scorpionic was too strong for the Power Rangers.

"Get ready, blockheads. You're all about to take a tumble."

"Zords alone won't defeat him," shouted the Red Ranger. "We have to combine forces!"

With all the Rangers in agreement, they combined into the Megazord!

Scorpionic rushed toward the Megazord, but was quickly pushed away. Enraged, Scorpionic slashed his sword at the Megazord.

Swiftly blocking the attack, the Megazord wielded its Katana blade.

Afraid that he would lose, Scorpionic called for backup. "Come, giant Moogers!"

Suddenly, a dozen giant Moogers sprang from Gaps and surrounded the Megazord. Armed with chains, the Moogers trapped the Megazord.

But even they are no match for the Megazord's Furious Lion Howl attack. A blast of fire shot out from the Megazord's armor plate and the giant Moogers exploded backward.

The Megazord then used the chains to lift the remaining Moogers into the air and smash them against one another.

Now that the Moogers were defeated, the Red Ranger said, "Let's squash this scorpion!"

"Katana power! Samurai Strike!" the Power Rangers called out.

With one mighty swing of their sword, Scorpionic was defeated in a huge explosion. All that was left of him were clouds of smoke.

With the rise of the Samurai Megazord, the Power Rangers triumphed and peace returned to our world . . . for now.